T0144948

Benny and the Fox

Author: Sally A. Berkes (Nan)
Illustrations by: Timothy Lohr

AuthorHouse™
1663 Liberty Drive
Bloomington, IN 47403
www.authorhouse.com
Phone: 1 (800) 839-8640

Published by AuthorHouse 06/18/2019

ISBN: 978-1-5462-7248-9 (sc)
978-1-5462-7931-0 (hc)
978-1-5462-7249-6 (e)

Library of Congress Control Number: 2018914774

Print information available on the last page.

author**HOUSE**®

This book belongs to, _____

From: "Nan" (grandmother Sally A. Berkes)

With Love,

WORDS FROM THE AUTHOR

What you might feel as disappointment sometimes,may very well be determination. You need to keep strong, keep focused and keep going.

Stumbling blocks are actually stepping stones. Take one step at a time and you can reach your goals whatever they may be.

Don't let others keep you from your goals.

If you have love in your heart,

You can be happy today

Benny and Mr. Fox

Benny is a Rottweiler dog, who lives in a house and likes to play ball in the yard

Mr. Fox lives in the woods behind Benny's house, and one day came to visit

"How do you know my name?" asked Benny

"I heard someone call your name,
over and over again."

"My name is Mr. Fox, I usually play at night"

"But one day I saw you and thought you just might...

Let me be your friend"

"We could just sit by your fence and chat.....

and talk about our day, or this and that"

"I really like you Benny. You are very kind to me."

"I like you too Mr. Fox, our friendship will always be"

"I will come back tomorrow
        and we will be together again"

Benny and Mr Fox have gone home for the night

The End

They'll have fun again tomorrow from morning 'til night.

To you my children Andrew and Jeffrey and to my grandchildren Kenzie and Bryan, and of course to any other grandchildren that may come along, if you are reading this, then I made it! Knowing that, remember whatever positive endeavors you want to pursue and challenges to face, let nothing and no one hold you back in any aspect of your life. Anything positive is possible.

To my children and grandchildren, remember I love you.

Love is everywhere! Find it, embrace it and share it.

Love,
Mom, MIL (better known as the Mother in Law) and of course me "Nan"

I thank my sons, Andrew and Jeffrey who have encouraged and supported me to continue in writing this fun story. How lucky to have the best daughters-in-law in the world Danielle and Kate and grandchildren in the world as well.

I thank my children Andrew and Jeffrey who encouraged me to continue in writing this fun story and who have supported me in every way.

It took a while to begin, but when the grandchildren were born, it got me started.

Of course Kudos to Timothy who worked diligently on the artistic works of this book. A challenge he must be proud of, as I am so thankful to him. THANK YOU TIM.

To the publishers who believed in me and stayed with me making it possible to complete this book - my first completed endeavor.

Printed in the United States
By Bookmasters